THE HOKEY HOKEY

Retold by NICHOLAS IAN

Illustrated by MISA SABURI

Music Arranged and Produced by
MUSICAL YOUTH PRODUCTIONS

CANTATA
LEARNING

WWW.CANTATALEARNING.COM

CANTATA LEARNING

Published by Cantata Learning
1710 Roe Crest Drive
North Mankato, MN 56003
www.cantatalearning.com

A note to educators and librarians from the publisher: Cantata Learning has provided the following data to assist in book processing and suggested use of Cantata Learning product.

Publisher's Cataloging-in-Publication Data
Prepared by Librarian Consultant: Ann-Marie Begnaud
Library of Congress Control Number: 2015958188
    The Hokey Hokey
    Series: Sing-along Songs : Action
    Retold by Nicholas Ian
    Illustrated by Misa Saburi
    Summary: Children will get their bodies moving by dancing and singing the Hokey Hokey! Full-color illustrations closely match the text to bring this classic song to life.
    ISBN: 978-1-63290-591-8 (library binding/CD)
    ISBN: 978-1-63290-631-1 (paperback/CD)
Suggested Dewey and Subject Headings:
    Dewey: E 398
    LCSH Subject Headings: Children's songs – Juvenile literature. | Nursery rhymes – Juvenile literature. | Anatomy – Juvenile literature. | Children's songs – Songs and music – Texts. | Nursery rhymes – Songs and music – Texts. | Anatomy – Songs and music – Texts. | Children's songs – Juvenile sound recordings. | Nursery rhymes – Juvenile sound recordings. | Anatomy – Juvenile sound recordings.
    Sears Subject Headings: Nursery Rhymes. | Human anatomy. | Human body. | School songbooks. | Children's songs. | World music.
    BISAC Subject Headings: JUVENILE FICTION / Nursery Rhymes. | JUVENILE FICTION / Stories in Verse. | JUVENILE FICTION / Concepts / Body.

Book design and art direction, Tim Palin Creative
Editorial direction, Flat Sole Studio
Music direction, Elizabeth Draper
Music arranged and produced by Musical Youth Productions

Printed in the United States of America in North Mankato, Minnesota.
122016   0357CGF16R

ACCESS THE MUSIC!

SCAN CODE WITH MOBILE APP

CANTATALEARNING.COM

Have you heard of the "Hokey Cokey"? This popular **British folk dance** is known around the world by other names. People call it the "Hokey Pokey" in the United States and Canada.

Now turn the page to get your body moving. Just be ready to sing and dance!

Left arm!

You put your left arm in,
your left arm out.
In, out, in, out,
you shake it all about.

You do the Hokey Hokey,
and you turn around.
That's what it's all about!

Right arm!

You put your right arm in,
your right arm out.
In, out, in, out,
you shake it all about.

You do the Hokey Hokey,
and you turn around.
That's what it's all about!

Whoa-oh, the Hokey Hokey.
Whoa-oh, the Hokey Hokey.
Whoa-oh, the Hokey Hokey.
Knees bent. Arms stretched.

Ra ra ra!

Left leg!

You put your left leg in,
your left leg out.
In, out, in, out,
you shake it all about.

You do the Hokey Hokey,
and you turn around.
That's what it's all about!

Right leg!

You put your right leg in,
your right leg out.
In, out, in, out,
you shake it all about.

You do the Hokey Hokey,
and you turn around.
That's what it's all about!

Whoa-oh, the Hokey Hokey.
Whoa-oh, the Hokey Hokey.
Whoa-oh, the Hokey Hokey.
Knees bent. Arms stretched.

Ra ra ra!

Whole self!

You put your whole self in, in!
Your whole self out, out!
In, out, in, out,
you shake it all about.

You do the Hokey Hokey,
and you turn around.
That's what it's all about!

Whoa-oh, the Hokey Hokey.
Whoa-oh, the Hokey Hokey.
Whoa-oh, the Hokey Hokey.
Knees bent. Arms stretched.

Ra ra ra!

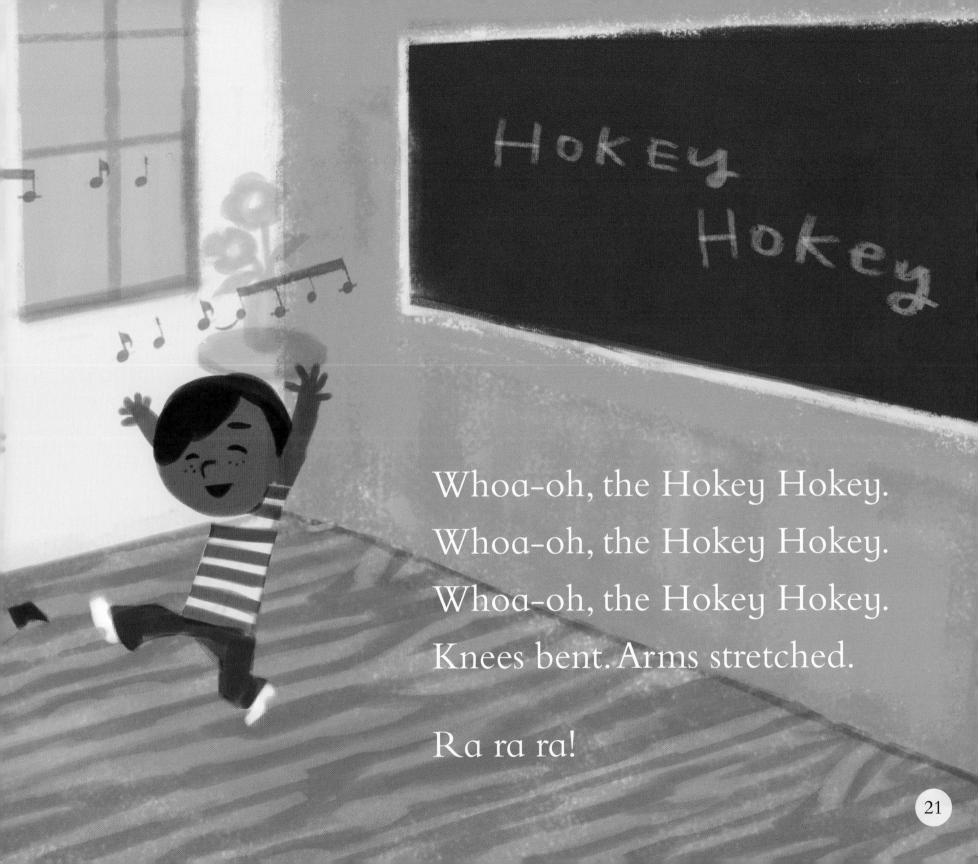

Whoa-oh, the Hokey Hokey.
Whoa-oh, the Hokey Hokey.
Whoa-oh, the Hokey Hokey.
Knees bent. Arms stretched.

Ra ra ra!

SONG LYRICS
Hokey Hokey

Left arm!

You put your left arm in,
your left arm out.
In, out, in, out,
you shake it all about.

You do the Hokey Hokey,
and you turn around.
That's what it's all about!

Right arm!

You put your right arm in,
your right arm out.
In, out, in, out,
you shake it all about.

You do the Hokey Hokey,
and you turn around.
That's what it's all about!

Whoa-oh, the Hokey Hokey.
Whoa-oh, the Hokey Hokey.
Whoa-oh, the Hokey Hokey.
Knees bent. Arms stretched.
Ra ra ra!

Left leg!

You put your left leg in,
your left leg out.
In, out, in, out,
you shake it all about.

You do the Hokey Hokey,
and you turn around.
That's what it's all about!

Right leg!

You put your right leg in,
your right leg out.
In, out, in, out,
you shake it all about.

You do the Hokey Hokey,
and you turn around.
That's what it's all about!

Whoa-oh, the Hokey Hokey.
Whoa-oh, the Hokey Hokey.
Whoa-oh, the Hokey Hokey.
Knees bent. Arms stretched.
Ra ra ra!

Whole self!

You put your whole self in, in!
Your whole self out, out!
In, out, in, out,
you shake it all about.

You do the Hokey Hokey,
and you turn around.
That's what it's all about!

Whoa-oh, the Hokey Hokey.
Whoa-oh, the Hokey Hokey.
Whoa-oh, the Hokey Hokey.
Knees bent. Arms stretched.
Ra ra ra!

Whoa-oh, the Hokey Hokey.
Whoa-oh, the Hokey Hokey.
Whoa-oh, the Hokey Hokey.
Knees bent. Arms stretched.
Ra ra ra!

Hokey Hokey

Indie Pop (Folk/World)
Musical Youth Productions

Verse

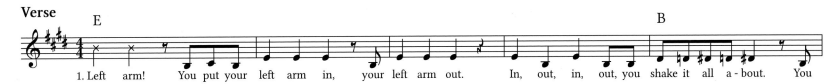

1. Left arm! You put your left arm in, your left arm out. In, out, in, out, you shake it all a-bout. You

do the Ho-key Ho-key, and you turn a-round. That's what it's all a-bout!

Verse 2
Right arm!
You put your right arm in, your right arm out.
In, out, in, out, you shake it all about.
You do the Hokey Hokey, and you turn around.
That's what it's all about!

Chorus

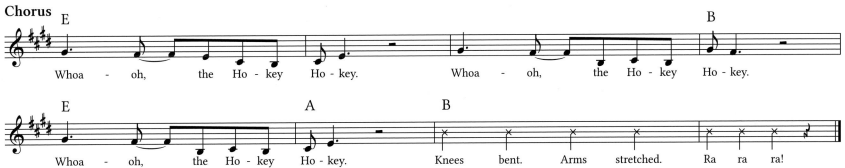

Whoa - oh, the Ho-key Ho-key. Whoa - oh, the Ho-key Ho-key.

Whoa - oh, the Ho-key Ho-key. Knees bent. Arms stretched. Ra ra ra!

Verse 3
Left leg!
You put your left leg in, your left leg out.
In, out, in, out, you shake it all about.
You do the Hokey Hokey, and you turn around.
That's what it's all about!

Verse 4
Right leg!
You put your right leg in, your right leg out.
In, out, in, out, you shake it all about.
You do the Hokey Hokey, and you turn around.
That's what it's all about!

Chorus

Verse 5
Whole self!
You put your whole self in, in! Your whole self out, out!
In, out, in, out, you shake it all about.
You do the Hokey Hokey, and you turn around.
That's what it's all about!

Chorus (x2)

GLOSSARY

British—from Great Britain, an island nation in Europe

folk dance—a traditional dance from a particular country or region

GUIDED READING ACTIVITIES

1. What is your favorite way to dance? Draw a picture of you and your friends dancing!

2. How many different body parts does this song mention? Can you think of any that the song doesn't mention?

3. Anyone can do the Hokey Hokey! Invite a friend, teacher, or parent to do the dance with you.

TO LEARN MORE

Anderson, Steven. *Happy and You Know It*. Minneapolis: Cantata Learning, 2016.

Long, Ethan. *The Croaky Pokey!* New York: Holiday House, 2011.

Rustad, Martha E. H. *My Body*. North Mankato, MN: Capstone Press, 2014.

Veitch, Catherine. *Dancing*. Chicago: Heinemann Library, 2010.